This edition published by Parragon Books Ltd in 2016 and distributed by

Parragon Inc.
440 Park Avenue South, 13th Floor
New York, NY 10016
www.parragon.com

Copyright © Parragon Books Ltd 2013-2016

Written by Margaret Wise Brown
Illustrated by Henry Fisher

Edited by Michael Diggle
Designed by Ailsa Cullen
Production by Jonathan Wakeham

ISBN 978-1-4748-5741-3

Printed in China

The Fish with the Deep Sea Smile

PaRRagon

Bath•New York•Cologne•Melbourne•Delhi
Hong Kong•Shenzhen•Singapore

They fished
and they fished,

Way down in the sea,

Down in the
sea a mile.

They fished among
all the fish in the sea,

For the fish with the
deep sea smile.

One fish came up
from the deep of the sea,

One fish came up
from the deep of the sea,
From down in the sea a mile,

With electric lights
up and down its tail,
But never a deep sea smile.

They fished
and they fished,
All across the sea,

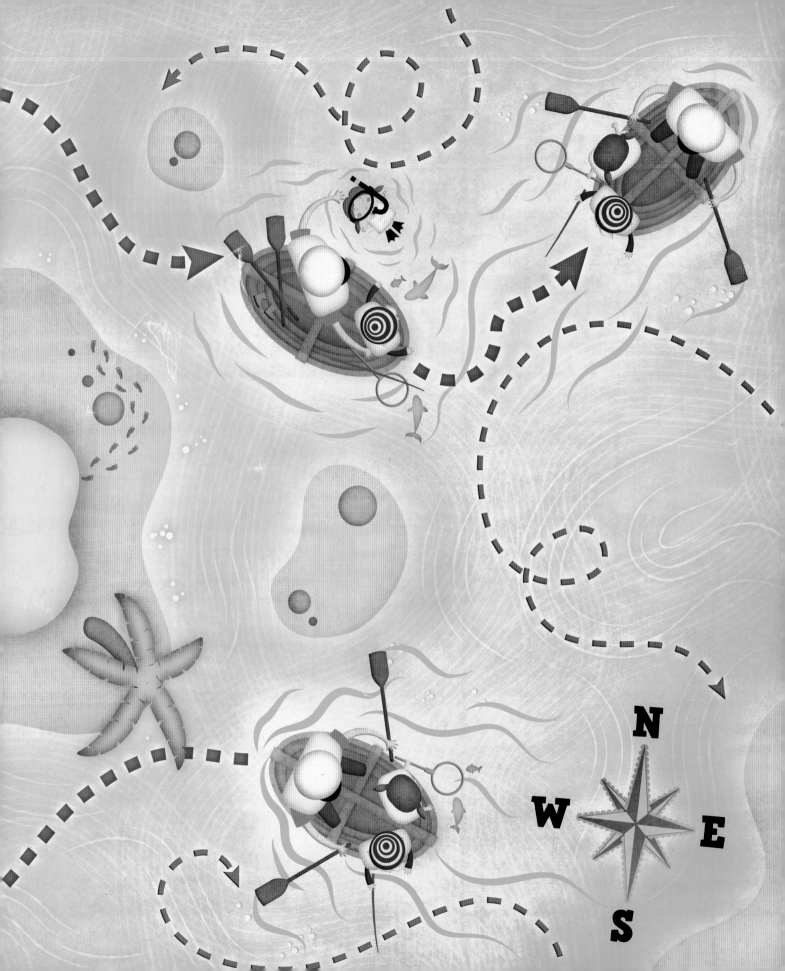

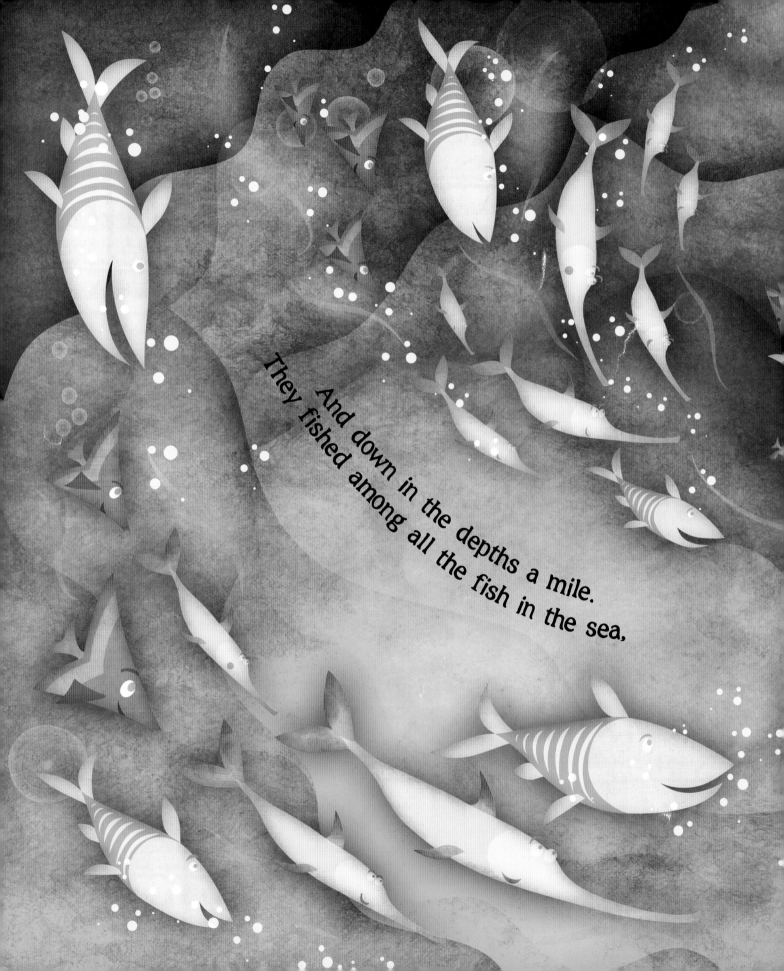

And down in the depths a mile.
They fished among all the fish in the sea,

For the fish with
the deep sea smile.

One fish came up with
terrible teeth,

One fish with a long strong jaw.

One fish came up with eyes on stalks,

One fish with terrible claws.

They fished all through the ocean deep,
For many and many a mile.

And then, one day,
they got a pull,

From down in the
sea a mile.

And when they pulled
the fish into the boat,

He smiled a
deep sea smile.

And as he smiled, the hook got free,
And then, what a deep sea smile!

He flipped his tail
and swam away,

Down in the sea a mile.